KU-750-700

For Mom and Dad—thank you for
helping me bloom. —A. S.

For Linus. —T. W.

STERLING CHILDREN'S BOOKS
New York

An Imprint of Sterling Publishing Co., Inc.
1166 Avenue of the Americas
New York, NY 10036

Text © 2017 by Annie Silvestro
Illustrations © 2017 by Teagan White

ISBN 978-1-4549-1632-1

Distributed in Canada by Sterling Publishing Co., Inc.
C/o Canadian Manda Group, 664 Annette Street
Toronto, Ontario, Canada M6S 2C8
Distributed in the United Kingdom by GMC Distribution Services
Castle Place, 166 High Street, Lewes, East Sussex, England BN7 1XU
Distributed in Australia by NewSouth Books
45 Beach Street, Coogee, NSW 2034, Australia

For information about custom editions, special sales, and premium and corporate purchases,
please contact Sterling Special Sales at 800-805-5489 or specialsales@sterlingpublishing.com.

Manufactured in China

Lot #:
2 4 6 8 10 9 7 5 3 1
07/17

sterlingpublishing.com

The artwork for this book was created using watercolor, gouache, and colored pencil.

Design by Irene Vandervoort

MICE SKATING

written by
ANNIE SILVESTRO

illustrated by
TEAGAN WHITE

STERLING CHILDREN'S BOOKS
New York

During the cold winter months,
most field mice take cover . . .

. . . tunneling deep underground,
burrowing into farmhouse walls,
nesting in hollow logs.

But not Lucy.
She loved the feeling of snow crunching
under her paws.

She loved how the frosty air made her whiskers freeze. And most of all, she loved wearing her fluffy wool hat with the pink pom-pom on top. It did more than keep her head warm. It kept her heart warm, too.

It made her brave.
It made her bold.
It made her bloom!

Lucy loved winter.
Her friends did not.

BRIE

PROVOLONE

"Your fur is freezing,"
said Mona when Lucy came inside.

"Your nose is dripping,"
said Millie.

"Your teeth are cheddar-ing!"
said Marcello.

"I know," said Lucy.
"Isn't it wonderful?"

She asked her friends to join her, but they wouldn't budge.
"We're comfy and cozy," they said, "warm and toasty till spring."
So Lucy donned her hat and dashed outside, all by herself.

She caught snowflakes with her tongue,
flapped her arms to make snow angels,
and built snowmice. **LOTS** of snowmice.
But Lucy wanted to share winter with her friends.

So she tried bringing it to them.
First she brought snow cones . . .

. . . then a giant icicle.

She even planned an indoor snowball fight.
It was a soggy flop.

"*PLEASE* come outside," begged Lucy.

"*Not till it's warm,*"
said Mona.

"*Not till the flowers bloom,*"
said Millie.

"*Not unless that snow
is made of mozzarella,*"
said Marcello.

One day, Lucy skidded on an ice patch.

She slipped. She slid.

She . . . soared!
Lucy couldn't wait to try again.

She fashioned skates out of pine needles
and scurried to the pond.

At first she wobbled.
She fell more than once.
But, with practice, soon she was ice skating.
Her tail twirled with joy.
She couldn't let her friends miss out on this!

So Lucy gathered supplies and
returned underground.

"Finally come to your senses?" asked Mona.
"Ready to thaw out?" squeaked Millie.
"Tired of being prov-alone?" asked Marcello.
Lucy hummed happily. "You'll see," she said.

Lucy skated every day.
Then she danced back to her burrow, trailing bits of
yarn or piles of pine needles.
The other mice wondered what she was doing.
But Lucy didn't say a word.
She just kept working quietly in her room.

Her friends grew more and more curious.
"What on earth are you up to?" asked Mona.
"Don't keep us in suspense," said Millie.
"We must pecori-know!" cried Marcello.

After a few finishing touches, Lucy was finally done.
She placed a new hat on each mouse's head.
"These will keep you warm," she said, "inside and out."
The mice marveled at their new hats.

"I have something else to show you," said Lucy. "Follow me."
And to her surprise, they did.

One by one the mice emerged from underground.
Lucy ushered them to the pond.
Then, as the sun twinkled across the ice, Lucy took off.

She spiraled and swirled,
swizzled and twizzled,
loop-de-looped.
She was flying!

"Marvelous!" cried Mona.
"Spectacular!" called Millie.
"Brie-vissimo!" cheered Marcello.
"We want to try!" squeaked her friends.

Lucy handed them their skates.
Then they teetered onto the ice.
They wobbled. They fell.
But with practice, soon they were mice skating.

"Wheeee!" squealed Mona.
"What fun!" squeaked Millie.
"Who knew winter could be so goud-a?" said Marcello.
"I did," said Lucy, beaming.
The mice cheered.

And together they bloomed like spring.